Z, BZZZZ, BZZZ

NNNNNNNNNNNNK!

GARGLE. GURGLE. GARGLE.

WHEWW

CRACKLE, POP,

CRACKLE, POP!

shooo, WOOOO,

shooooo, WOOOOO

Bounce, bounce, bounce.

THRRIP.
ZOOP.
THRRRR
slooop slooop
brrrmp.
brrrmp.
brrrmp.
buh buh
RUNCH.
UNCH.

# Daddy's Favorite "SOUND"

Brock Eastman and Kinley Eastman | Illustrated by David Miles

HARVEST KIDS

HARVEST HOUSE PUBLISHERS
EUGENE, OREGON

The Scripture verse at the end of the story is from the New King James Version®. Copyright © 1982 by Thomas Nelson, Inc. Used by permission. All rights reserved.

Cover design by Mary Eakin

Interior design by Left Coast Design

Published in association with the Steve Laube Agency, LLC, 24 W. Camelback Rd. A-635, Phoenix, Arizona 85013.

HARVEST KIDS is a trademark of The Hawkins Children's LLC. Harvest House Publishers, Inc., is the exclusive licensee of the trademark HARVEST KIDS.

## Daddy's Favorite Sound

Copyright © 2019 by Brock Eastman
Artwork © 2019 by David Miles
Published by Harvest House Publishers
Eugene, Oregon 97408
www.harvesthousepublishers.com

ISBN 978-0-7369-7474-5 (hardcover)

Library of Congress Cataloging-in-Publication Data

Names: Eastman, Brock, 1983- author. | Eastman, Kinley, 2009- | Miles, David, 1973- illustrator.
Title: Daddy's favorite sound / Brock Eastman and Kinley Eastman; illustrated by David Miles.
Description: Eugene, Oregon: Harvest House Publishers, [2019] | Summary: Illustrations and easy-to-read text follow Little Lion and Daddy Lion through their day, as Little Lion anxiously tries to find her father's favorite sound. Includes a prayer and directions for making maracas.
Identifiers: LCCN 2018025290 | ISBN 9780736974745 (hardback)
Subjects: | CYAC: Fathers and daughters—Fiction. | Sound—Fiction. | Love—Fiction. | Lions—Fiction. | Christian life—Fiction. | BISAC: JUVENILE NONFICTION / Religious / Christian / Early Readers.
Classification: LCC PZ7.E126774 Dad 2019 | DDC [E]—dc23 LC record available at https://lccn.loc.gov/2018025290

**All rights reserved.** No part of this publication may be reproduced, stored in a retrieval system, or transmitted in any form or by any means—electronic, mechanical, digital, photocopy, recording, or any other—except for brief quotations in printed reviews, without the prior permission of the publisher.

**Printed in China**

18 19 20 21 22 23 24 25 26 / LP / 10 9 8 7 6 5 4 3 2 1

**Brock**

To my wife, without whom I'd never get to hear, "I love you, Daddy."
And to my kids, who know how to make my favorite sound.

**Kinley**

To Mae Mae, Waves, and Deckledoo, because I love you.
And my cat, Blue Belle Pumpkin, because I love you too.

**David**

To my sister, Carrie. My work in this book would
not exist without your encouragement.
I miss you so much.

Little Lion flung open the door, dashed into the room, and blew her whistle with all her might.

WHEWWW, WHEWWW, WHEWWWW

Daddy Lion grumbled and roared and sat up in bed.

Little Lion smiled and asked, "Daddy, Daddy, is this your favorite sound?"

Daddy shook his head.

"A whistle isn't my favorite sound."

"Then Daddy, Daddy,
        where can it be found?"

"Little Lion, to find it, you'll
        have to look around!"

As daddy flipped pancakes in a pan, Little Lion began to slurp her milk as loud as she could.

Sloop, slurp, slurrrp.

And then she asked, "Daddy, Daddy, is this your favorite sound?"

Daddy flipped a pancake onto her plate and said,
  "Slurping milk is too silly to be my favorite sound."

"Then Daddy, Daddy,
  where can it be found?"

"Little Lion, to find it,
  you'll have to look around."

Little Lion pawed through her toy box, looking for things that make unusual sounds. She spotted her slinky and began moving it from paw to paw.

**THRRIP, ZOOP, THRRRRIP.**

Had she found Daddy Lion's favorite sound?

She jumped on his lap and asked,
"Daddy, Daddy, is this your favorite sound?"

Daddy leaned in close and listened.

"That's interesting indeed...
but not my favorite sound."

"Then Daddy, Daddy,
where can it be found?"

"Little Lion, to find it,
you'll have to look around."

The Lion family was off to the store, and this gave Little Lion an idea. She climbed into the front seat of the car and pressed the horn as hard as she could.

HONK, HONNNK HONNNNNNNN

Little Lion smiled.
"Daddy, Daddy, is this your favorite sound?"

Daddy Lion shook his head while Baby Lion covered his ears.
"No, a honking horn is too loud to be my favorite sound."
"Then Daddy, Daddy, where can it be found?"

"Little Lion, to find it, you'll have to look around."

Little Lion always rode the mechanical horse after her family finished shopping. She climbed up and put in a penny. As it galloped she hummed,

b<sup>r</sup>r<sub>r</sub>mp,
b<sup>r</sup>r<sub>r</sub>mp,
b<sup>r</sup>r<sub>r</sub>mp,
buh buh.

And then she asked,
"Daddy, Daddy, is this
your favorite sound?"

As the ride ended, Daddy Lion lifted Little Lion off.

"A horse racing isn't my favorite sound."

"Then Daddy, Daddy, where can it be found?"

"Little Lion, to find it, you'll have to look around."

When they got home, Little Lion still hadn't found Daddy Lion's favorite sound. While Daddy washed the car, Little Lion bounced her favorite ball.

Bounce, bounce, bounce.

Daddy loved playing ball with her.
Maybe this was his favorite sound!

Little Lion bounced the ball quickly and asked,
"Daddy, Daddy, is this your favorite sound?"

Little Lion passed the ball
to Daddy, and he bounced
it several times
and listened.

"No, Little Lion, this
isn't my favorite
sound."

"Then Daddy, Daddy,
where can it be found?"

"Little Lion, to find it, you'll have to look around."

Daddy Lion and Little Lion climbed up to the treehouse for a picnic lunch.
As they sat eating their sandwiches and vegetables, Little Lion
crunched down on a carrot stick.

CRUNCH.
CRUNCH.
CRUNCH.

Little Lion gasped. Daddy Lion loved carrots!
"Daddy, Daddy, is this your favorite sound?"

Daddy Lion stuck two carrots on his fangs, making him look like Mr. Walrus from down the street.

"I do love carrots, but crunching them doesn't make my favorite sound."

"Then Daddy, Daddy, where can it be found?"

"Little Lion, to find it, you'll have to look around."

Daddy pushed Little Lion on her swing,
and the wind swept through her fur.

Shooo, woooo,
shoooooo, woooooooo!

Swinging was something she and Daddy loved to do together.
"Daddy, Daddy, does the wind make your favorite sound?"

His thick brown mane blew wildly in the air.

"No, Little Lion, the chilly wind doesn't
make my favorite sound."

"Then Daddy, Daddy,
where can it be found?"

"Little Lion, to find it,
you'll have to look around."

Little Lion spent the rest of the afternoon trying different sounds.

# BZZZ, BZZZZ, BZZZZZZ.

Was it the *buzz* of Daddy's mane trimmer?

### CRACKLE, POP, CRACKLE, POP!

The *crackle* and *pop* of fire in the fireplace?

### Drip, drop, drip, drop, drip, drop.

Maybe it was the *drip, drop* of his coffee maker.

Again and again Little Lion asked,
   "Daddy, is *this* your favorite sound?"

And again and again,
   Daddy Lion replied,

      "No, Little Lion, that is not
      my favorite sound."

THRRRIP

      "Then Daddy, Daddy, where can it be found?"

      "Little Lion, to find it, you'll have to look around."

Still Little Lion had not found Daddy's favorite sound, and after dinner it would be time for bed.

CLAP, CLAP, CLAP.

As Daddy finished praying before their meal,
Baby Lion began to clap.

Daddy Lion smiled. "Thank you."

Little Lion perked up.
"Daddy, Daddy, is clapping your
favorite sound?" She clapped
her paws a couple of times.

Daddy Lion shook his head.
"No, Little Lion, clapping
isn't my favorite sound."

"Then Daddy, Daddy,
where can it be found?"

"Little Lion, to find it,
you'll have to look around."

"Daddy, Daddy, is this your favorite sound?"

Little Lion sipped some mouthwash
   from a cup and swished it in her mouth.

# GARGLE, GURGLE, GARGLE.

"Your breath is minty fresh,
   but gargling isn't my favorite sound."

"Then Daddy, Daddy, where can it be found?"

"Little Lion, to find it, you'll have to look around."

Little Lion had not found Daddy Lion's favorite sound,
and since it was time for bed, her search had to come to an end.

"Daddy, Daddy,
I love you,"

Little Lion said as she hugged Daddy Lion.
"Can you tell me? What's your favorite sound?"

"You just made it,"
Daddy Lion said.

"Words?" Little Lion asked.

Daddy Lion gave her a wink.
"Special words."

"I love you?"
Little Lion asked.

Daddy Lion grinned.
"*That* is my favorite sound."

Daddy Lion leaned over and
kissed Little Lion's forehead.

**"And I love you."**

We love Him because He first loved us.

*1 John 4:19*

When we say "I love you" and show love through our actions, we reflect Jesus. As He loved us, so we love Him and show His love to others.

### Prayer

Jesus, thank You for telling me You love me. I want to tell others about Your love. I love You, Jesus. Amen.

### Questions to Ask Your Child

What is your favorite sound?

Who do you say "I love you" to?

What is your favorite thing to do with someone you love?

## An Activity to Do with Your Child

*Making Maracas*

   *Supplies*

      White or brown rice

      Empty plastic Easter eggs

      Plastic spoons

      Tape

   *Steps*

   1. Pour the rice into one half of the empty plastic Easter egg.
   2. Close up the Easter egg.
   3. Wrap a piece of tape around the egg to secure it.
   4. Place the heads of two plastic spoons on either side of the egg.
   5. Wrap tape around the spoon heads and egg, securing them together.
   6. Tape the bottom of the spoon handles together.
   7. Let your child shake it and make music!

**Brock Eastman** is the author of the Quest for Truth series, the Imagination Station series Showdown with the Shepherd, and the Hippopolis series. He writes for *Clubhouse* and *Clubhouse Jr.* magazines and often speaks to schools and writing groups. Brock currently works for Compassion International, whose mission is to release kids from poverty worldwide. www.brockeastman.com

**Kinley Eastman** stood in her playroom with a slinky and asked her daddy, "Is this your favorite sound?" She loves reading and hopes this is just the first of many books to be published. www.kinleyeastman.com

**David Miles** has been blessed to illustrate for many amazing publishers. He has worked on numerous children's books, book covers, magazine articles, puzzles, games, and more Bible stories than he can keep track of! David is currently working full-time as an illustrator and is probably drawing right now! You can see more of his work at **www.davidmiles.us**.

Join Little Lion and her family as the fun
continues in *Mommy's Favorite Smell.*

CLAP, CLAP, CLAP, BZ

HONK, HONNNK, HO

WHEWWW, WHEW

SLOOP, THRRIP,

brrrmp,
brrrmp,
brrrmp,
buh buh.

ZOOP,

THRRR

CRUNCH,
CRUNCH,

slurp, slurrrp,

Drip, drop, drip, drop, drip, drop,